ADAM HOLWICK

Chaotic tales of fear and death

Contents

Acknowledgement

I want to thank Carl McRaven for the killer cover art (pun intended) he designed for this book.

And also, my beta readers and editor for helping me to make this book the best it can be, yall are awesome, and I love ya for that.

1

The Bloody Mary Challenge

Michael and Jason had been friends since fifth grade and attended the same middle school. On Halloween night, Michael was at Jason's house, where they spent the evening watching scary movies. After watching a scary movie, Jason suggested they play a game called the Bloody Mary Challenge. Unfamiliar with this game, Michael asked what it was. Jason explained that they would take turns going into the en-suite bathroom in his room with only a candle for light. Then they would have to look into the mirror and say "Bloody Mary" three times. If they did it right, she should appear in the mirror.

After taking a moment to consider, Michael agreed, and the boys played a round of rock, paper, scissors to see who would go first. To Michael's disappointment, he lost. After calming his nerves, he lit a candle and entered the bathroom, closing the door behind him. There was an eerie vibe, with the candle being the only light.

Michael put the candle on the counter and stared at his

reflection in the mirror. Then he began the challenge.

"Bloody Mary, Bloody Mary, Bloody Mar—"

Before he could finish, the candle blew out, leaving him in total darkness. Then he heard a woman scream directly in his ear.

Michael scrambled frantically to find the doorknob, flung the door open, and ran out, panting When Jason asked what happened, Michael told him everything. Unnerved by what had happened, the boys ended the game and went to bed, leaving the light on.

The next evening, after Michael finished his homework, he went into his bathroom to brush his teeth and get ready for bed. When he brushed his teeth, he looked into the mirror, remembering the previous night's events. Suddenly, a dark-haired woman in a white dress covered in blood appeared behind him in the mirror. Startled, Michael spun around – but found nobody there. Taking a moment to calm himself, he put the incident out of his mind and went to bed.

A week had passed. The blood-covered woman in the mirror showed up in Michael's dreams several times, but Michael kept these incidents to himself. One night, during his usual nighttime routine, the blood-covered woman appeared again in the mirror. This time, the woman lunged at him *through* the mirror before Michael could react, ripping his throat out and tearing into his stomach, leaving him in a pool of blood on the floor.

The following day, Michael's mother found him dead and, in a panic, called the police.

Several weeks passed, and the police still had no leads in the case. It remains a cold case to this day.

2

Ouija Nightmare

One Halloween night, two high-school girls, Sandra and Lacy, were out having fun and decided to sneak into the local cemetery with an Ouija board to perform a session. After walking around for a bit, the girls found a dark spot that would allow them to remain hidden from view should anyone walk by.

After setting up the board and lighting a few candles, the girls sat down and placed their hands on the planchette. Taking a breath to calm herself, Sandra asked if any spirits were there that would like to speak to them. A few seconds passed, then the planchette jerked quickly to the word "yes" on the board. Surprised, Sandra looked at Lacy and accused her of moving it, which Lacy denied. Taking a moment to calm down, Sandra asked if they were speaking to a boy or girl; after a short pause, the planchette spelled out "unknown." Sandra asked how many spirits were present. Again, there was a brief pause, then the planchette jerked to the number 1 and then the 3.

A cold breeze blew through the cemetery, and the candles went out. The girls continued the session without wanting to take their hands off the planchette.

Without thinking before she spoke, Sandra asked if she and Lacy were in danger. There was a long pause; then the planchette pointed to "yes."

Sandra experienced an intense burning feeling on her back. When she lifted her shirt for Lacy to see, Lacy told her there were three claw marks on her back.

Frightened, the girls ran out of the cemetery, leaving the board and candles behind. Shaken by the night's events, they walked back to their homes together, feeling fortunate they lived across the street from each other, so neither would have to walk alone. Once she got home, Sandra decided to take a bath before going to bed.

Sandra wasn't at school the next day, so Lacy went to her house after classes ended. Responding to her knock, Sandra opened the door, looking like she hadn't slept in weeks. She said she had a horrible nightmare about a creepy woman with dark hair, red eyes, and pale white skin chasing her. After talking briefly, the girls realized they had left the board in the cemetery and hadn't closed it properly.

That evening, Lacy returned to where they had performed the session. She was alone, as Sandra refused to go back. She found everything right where they had left them. With relief, she gathered everything in her bag and took it home.

A week went by, and Sandra still hadn't returned to school. Concerned, Lacy went to Sandra's house to check on her. Sandra's mother answered the door. When Lacy asked how Sandra was doing, her mother explained that she was sick and too weak to leave the bed. When Lacy asked if she could see her, Sandra's mother agreed and led her to Sandra's room.

Lacy found Sandra lying in bed, looking very pale, with dark circles under her eyes and a weak smile at seeing her best friend. As she was too weak to talk much, Lacy sat beside Sandra and told her about what she had missed at school the past week. After a while, Lacy said goodbye and told her friend to try and get some rest.

The following day, Lacy's mom came into her room with her eyes full of tears and told her that Sandra's mom had just called and that Sandra had died during the night. Heartbroken, Lacy collapsed on the floor and began crying.

Sandra's cause of death was stated as a heart attack, and the case was closed.

After Sandra's funeral, Lacy went to her room, pulled out the Ouija board, performed a cleansing ceremony she had learned to seal it, then locked it away in a drawer. No other events occurred after the cleansing, and Lacy never used the board again.

3

Eyes of Evil

Lucas would often spend his evenings at home alone, as his mother worked shifts from six to six in the morning at the hospital. It was just the two of them in their single-story family home, as his father had taken off before he was born.

One night, Lucas was watching TV in the living room when he heard a knock on the door. He turned on the porch light and looked out the window beside the front door to see a girl wearing a gray hoodie and blue jeans, who looked around thirteen or so, standing outside on the porch. Still looking out the window, Lucas asked what she wanted. She turned to look directly at him and asked if she could come inside to call her father because he was supposed to pick her up but had never come.

At this point, Lucas noticed her eyes were both entirely black, and her face was white as a sheet. Terrified, Lucas denied her request and asked her to leave, then ran into his bedroom as quickly as possible. A few minutes later, he heard banging on his bedroom window. When he looked over, he saw the girl standing there, pounding on the window and glaring at him. The girl screamed at him to let her in, still beating on the window. Again, Lucas refused and yelled at her to go away, and then he covered his ears and began repeating The Lord's prayer. The girl hissed at him and ran off.

The rest of the night passed peacefully. The following day, Lucas told his mother what had happened. She was unsettled by what Lucas told her and went to their neighbor's house to ask if they had heard or had seen anything unusual during the night, but none of them had seen or heard anything.

A few days passed. Once again, Lucas was home alone, playing video games in the living room. At around 8 PM, there was a knock on the door. It was the same girl.

Before Lucas could speak, the girl apologized for frightening him, dropped her hood, and smiled at him, her black eyes gleaming. She asked if he wanted to come out and play. Feeling slightly better at seeing her smile, Lucas agreed. He put his shoes on and opened the door.

The moment he stepped outside, the girl lunged at him, and the two vanished without a trace.

The following day, Lucas's mother returned home to find the front door wide open. She ran inside to look for Lucas but found nothing and called the police. When they arrived, they took her statement and said they would open an investigation and start looking for Lucas.

Weeks passed, and the police called off the search. Lucas was never seen again and was classified by the police as a runaway.

4

Terror in the Dark

It was the summer of 2009, and Tom and his friends Sara, James, and Mark went on a camping trip to Mt. Hood National Forest to celebrate their college graduation. They spent their days swimming in the lake and drinking, and at night they drank and made s'mores.

One night, while they were around the campfire, they heard a loud howl, unlike any wolves or coyotes native to the area. Startled, Sara grabbed a flashlight and scanned the tree line, looking for movement, but found nothing. Rattled by what they had heard, they decided to go inside the RV they had rented for the trip and go to bed.

A couple of hours before sunrise, the group was awakened by rustling and growling noises from outside. From the window of the RV, They could make out what appeared to be a large, hairy creature on two legs, rummaging through their campsite. When the creature looked in their direction, they saw glowing red eyes before it ran off into the woods.

Unable to sleep, the group decided to stay up for the rest of the night. After sunrise, they emerged from their RV and found their campsite a complete mess, with large animal footprints all over the ground.

After discussing it, the group agreed it was best not to push their luck. They returned to the RV and left, vowing never to return to the campsite or speak of what they had seen ever again.

5

The Devil of the Pine Barrens

It was a hot summer day in Chatsworth, New Jersey, when Scott and his girlfriend Lisa, visiting from out of town, were having lunch on a campsite in the Pine Barrens. While they were eating, Scott told Lisa, a local legend.

"Legend has it that the Pine Barrens are home to a terrifying creature called the Jersey Devil. Some also call it the Leeds Devil as it is believed to be the cursed thirteenth offspring of Mother Leeds."

Unimpressed, Lisa shrugged him off, assuming he was trying to scare her.

Taking her skepticism as a challenge, Scott suggested they spend the weekend out in the Pine Barrens to prove what he told her was true. She accepted, and the two continued eating lunch, talking, and having a good time.

That weekend, the couple went shopping for the things they

would need. After a short drive, they parked the car and began their hike up to the campsite. They could hear many different birds in the trees, but nothing out of the ordinary. Just after 1 PM, they arrived at the campsite, set up their tent and chairs, and then made lunch. Lisa jokingly remarked that she still hadn't seen proof of the Jersey Devil, but Scott smiled and told her to give it time.

The day passed uneventfully. After dinner, they were sitting enjoying the campfire and talking when they heard a strange sound, unlike any animal they knew. Unable to figure out what they had heard, the couple disregarded it and went to bed.

The following day, when the couple came out of their tent, they found hoof and claw marks on the ground around the campsite. Still skeptical, Lisa accused Scott of setting it up, which he denied.

The day was mostly quiet, with nothing but the usual birds chirping and other sounds of nature. That evening, as the sun was setting, they heard the same strange sound they had heard the previous day. However, when they looked above the trees this time, they saw a large creature with goat-like legs, long arms, claws on its five-fingered hands, massive bat-like wings, and a head resembling a horse flying in a circle overhead.

Terrified, they ran for the trail, leaving behind their camping gear. As they ran, they realized the creature was flying directly behind them. They were exhausted when they finally reached Scott's car, and after frantically trying to grab his keys, he managed to unlock the car, and they both jumped in and drove away as fast as they could.

After a few minutes, they noticed they were no longer being followed and slowed down.

The next day, Scott moved in with Lisa in Colorado, and they never returned to the New Jersey Pine Barrens again.

6

Voices from Beyond the Grave

Allie was your average young adult, except since she was a child, she had been plagued with seeing and hearing people others could not. Her family told her it was a gift passed down through her father's side and sometimes skipped a generation, as her father did not have it. After college, she moved to Albuquerque, New Mexico, to begin a job as a sound tech for a local TV station. She moved into her new house on a Saturday, and her first day at work wasn't until Monday. It was evening when Allie finished unpacking, at which point she was tired and didn't feel like making dinner, so she ordered pizza. After about half an hour, she heard a knock on her door. After eating her pizza, Allie put her leftovers in the refrigerator and went to her bathroom to shower and get ready for bed.

Afterward, she heard voices screaming at her from the hallway. Annoyed, Allie turned to her open bedroom door and yelled, "Shut the fuck up!" The voices silenced, then she got into bed and went to sleep.

The day was bright and sunny, so Allie changed into her gym clothes and jogged around the block. Not long into her jog, she saw a man covered in blood watching her, but after a moment, she realized it was just one of her visions and continued jogging.

An hour later, Allie returned home, exhausted. While showering, she heard several voices making rude and inappropriate comments about her. Not wanting to deal with it because she was too tired, Allie sighed, ignored them, and finished her shower. Afterward, she got dressed and went about her day in peace.

Early the following day, Allie was in the kitchen making breakfast when one of the cabinets behind her opened and closed by itself. She looked behind her, growled, "That's enough!" and resumed cooking.

It was a long first day at work, and Allie was happy to be back home. When she entered the house, she went directly to her bedroom, changed into sweats and a T-shirt, and then settled on the living room couch to watch TV. A couple of hours passed, and she began to get sleepy, so she got up and went to bed.

Around 3 AM, Allie was awakened by a loud crash from the kitchen. When she arrived, she found the cabinets open and saw that several glasses had been smashed on the floor. Now very angry, Allie screamed, "Fucking assholes!" and grabbed a broom to clean up the mess. Once she had finished cleaning, she calmed down a bit and went back to bed.

The next day was peaceful, and the workday passed smoothly.

Once Allie got home, she went through her usual routine of changing into her sweats and T-shirt and watching TV. She was lying on the couch, flipping through channels, and suddenly felt cold air beside her head. When she turned to look, she saw a woman with black eyes and long dark hair looking down at her. Before Allie could react, the woman grabbed her by the hair, dragged her off the couch and across the room, and vanished.

Frustrated, Allie called her father, told him what had happened, and asked for advice. Her father told her he would call a family friend who could help and asked Allie to remain calm so that whatever was there couldn't feed off her fears.

The following day, Allie was sitting in her kitchen having her morning coffee when she heard a knock at the door. When she opened the door, she found an older-looking lady who seemed to be in her fifties, who Allie recognized as the family friend her father had spoken of. The woman introduced herself as Lady Miranda, a Wiccan priestess who had been her father's friend since they were kids.

Relieved to see her, Allie invited Lady Miranda inside and told her about everything happening. Lady Miranda told her she could help and would teach Allie some techniques to guard herself against these spirits and cleanse the house so they wouldn't return.

After an hour of training to help Allie guard herself, they began to cleanse the home of its negative energy using sage and prayers. As they did this, the activity in the house started again, and Allie heard voices screaming and cursing at them all at once.

Seeing this activity rattled Allie, Lady Miranda encouraged her to use the techniques she had learned to block them out. As Allie tried to do so, several spirits appeared around them, still screaming and cursing. Then another entity appeared to Allie, standing with the others, but this one wasn't human, and it was dark and menacing. Allie heard it speaking to her, but its lips didn't move. Over and over, the entity told her to kill the woman performing the prayers and to give in to them.

Her head pounding from the strain, Allie collapsed on the floor. Lady Miranda stopped her prayers and knelt to check on her. Suddenly, Allie lifted her head, but her eyes were now black as coal, and she had an evil grin. Before Lady Miranda could react, Allie lunged at her and began to strangle her. After a few minutes, Lady Miranda's body went limp and lay motionless on the floor.

The entity and all the spirits surrounding Allie vanished, and she regained her senses. Seeing what she had done, she screamed in panic. After a few minutes, she calmed down and decided to call the police and turn herself in.

Allie's trial ended with a verdict of insanity, and she was sent to a mental hospital. She never again heard or saw the entity or any other spirits, and now she spends her days silently staring at the walls of her room, never speaking to anyone.

7

The Deal

Josh had always dreamed of being a track and field star, but since birth, he had been plagued with lung issues. A few days after his twelfth birthday, he was relaxing and playing guitar in the garage with the door open when an older-looking man approached him. He introduced himself as Mr. Scratch and said he was a track and field manager looking for promising talent to manage. Josh sighed and told the man he couldn't play sports due to lung issues. Mr. Scratch smiled, pulled a contract from his coat, and said he could make all that disappear; all Josh had to do was sign the contract. Skeptical but intrigued, Josh signed the contract without reading it.

The following day, Josh awoke and immediately noticed that he felt stronger than ever, and his breathing was Clear for the first time in his life.

A few days later, he tried out for the school track and field team and dominated the tryouts.

By his senior year, Josh had won multiple first-place trophies and was offered a scholarship to UCLA, which he accepted. Josh was named MVP on his 21st birthday. Two weeks later, he had an unexpected visit from a familiar figure. Mr. Scratch had come to pay a visit.

Dispensing with the pleasantries, Mr. Scratch got right to the point. He had come to collect on Josh's contract and told Josh he owed him his soul.

Annoyed, Josh brushed him off and told Mr. Scratch to get lost. As Josh turned away, he felt a sharp pain in his chest and fell to the floor. Just before he lost consciousness, Josh saw Mr. Scratch standing over him, his eyes glowing red.

The next day, one of Josh's teammates came to Josh's dorm room to find him dead on the floor. The autopsy determined that he had suffered a fatal asthma attack.

A week later, after his funeral, the track team held a private memorial to remember their teammate and friend.

8

Shadows

Blake was a Registered Nurse and had just been hired at a skilled nursing facility in Phoenix, Arizona. The facility had been built back in the fifties. On Blake's first day, he was told that the last nurse who had worked there had left, claiming the place was haunted. Blake shrugged it off, as he didn't believe in the paranormal.

One day, Blake was asked if he could cover night shifts once a week, to which he agreed to break up the day-to-day routine. Little did he know what he was in for.

Blake's first night started fairly typical; most of his patients were asleep, so he didn't need to do much. At about 3 AM, Blake was doing his rounds when he noticed a dark shadow slowly moving along the hall and into one of his patients' rooms. Curious, Blake followed it but found nothing inside, and the patient was fast asleep. As he was about to turn and walk away, the patient started gasping for air and grabbing his chest as if in pain. Alarmed, Blake called for help and told the nurse at the desk to call for an ambulance. Unfortunately, the patient died just as the ambulance arrived.

After the commotion died down, the rest of the night passed peacefully.

The following day, after giving his notes to his replacement, Blake went to talk with the head of nursing and told them what had happened. After listening to his report, the head of nursing told Blake that it was nothing to be concerned about and to put it out of his mind.

The following week, Blake's weekly night shift started peacefully again; this time, nothing happened, and his shift passed without any problems.

Blake had a day off work the next day, and he decided to research the shadowy figure he had seen on his first night shift. After sifting through numerous websites and witness accounts, he found information suggesting that shadow people were believed to be dark entities that preyed on the living.

A week passed, and Blake arrived for his night shift. As usual, it was quiet for the first few hours, but at 3 AM, Blake was sitting alone at the nurses' station when he noticed movement out of the corner of his eye. When he turned to look, he saw the same shadow figure as before, but this time it seemed to be looking at him. After a few seconds, the figure raised its hand, and its fingers grew like black tentacles coming right at Blake.

Terrified, Blake jumped out of his chair, grabbed his backpack, and ran out of the building. The next day he resigned and moved away, never to return.

9

Dark Seance

Since freshman year of high school, Raven had always been interested in magic and seances and was nicknamed "creepy chick" by her fellow students. It was probably meant to be insulting, but Raven liked it and would smile when people called her that. She studied magic and other paranormal things, though she never actively tried them until she moved out of her parent's home and went to college. She started with stuff like summoning Bloody Mary in the mirror, but one day she decided it was time to try something more. She went to a local shop that sold antiques, where she found a crystal ball on sale, which she bought along with a large cloth adorned with a pentagram and a Celtic knot design.

Raven researched how to perform a seance and crystal ball scrying on her computer. After a few weeks, she felt confident enough that she knew what she was doing to give it a try.

After sundown, Raven cleared a space on the floor and laid out the cloth she had purchased, with the pentagram's top point facing north, and she set the crystal ball in the center. She lit some candles, then sat on the floor, taking a breath to calm herself. Then she asked if any spirits would like to speak with her, show themselves in the crystal ball, or make a noise. After an hour without results, Raven closed the session and went to bed.

Raven tried to communicate with spirits each night, and it was always the same: no results.

This went on for about a week. One night, after Raven closed her session, she decided to shower before bed to clear her head and consider what she may be doing wrong. As she was washing her hair, she heard a voice whispering her name in her ear. Startled, she turned off the shower and covered herself with the towel on the rack. Then she checked around her dorm nervously but found she was the only one there. Unable to sleep, Raven stayed up the rest of the night.

Raven had no classes the following day, so she visited a bookstore near her campus to look for books about demons and cleansing rituals. Luckily, they had one such book in stock, which she had purchased. She returned to her dorm to rest and read the book.

Over the next week, the activity continued to escalate while Raven attempted to clear the negative energy. One night, as she was brushing her teeth, she saw her face in the bathroom mirror morph into a frightening creature with horns and sharp fangs. Startled, she tripped and fell to the floor.

The next day in class, as Raven listened to the lecture, she kept hearing a voice inside her head insulting her, calling her a freak, and mocking her that it would eventually get her. Raven did her best to ignore these taunts and was relieved when classes ended for the day.

After reaching her dorm, Raven made some tea and sat at her desk to work on her assignments. As she worked, the bathroom door slammed behind her. Terrified by the sudden noise, Raven screamed and spilled hot tea on her hand, giving her a slight burn, but nothing too serious. Once she had calmed down, she put her cup down, took a first aid kit from her desk drawer, and applied ointment on her hand to soothe the pain.

Just as she was about to return to work, the teacup rose from her desk and flew past her, missing her head by inches and shattering against the door. Too frightened to sleep, Raven lay awake for the rest of the night.

These occurrences continued for several days, leaving Raven physically and mentally drained due to lack of sleep.

While performing her sage cleansing one night, Raven heard an evil-sounding laugh inside her head. The harder she tried to block it out, the louder it got, and then it turned from laughing to mocking her, saying it had won and that she should give up. As Raven resisted, the voice repeated things like "Give in" and "You can't win."

After several minutes of struggling to remain in control, Raven's will finally broke. The demon took control of her body, making her grab the knife she used for rituals she had been studying and cut her own throat.

The next day, Raven's body was found lying in a pool of blood on the floor, still clutching the knife. The police soon closed their investigation, labeling her death as suicide.

10

Witch of the Woods

Kevin was a grad student from South Dakota working towards his master's Degree in paleontology. While on spring vacation, he decided to go camping in the woods of the Black Hills. The first night was quiet; Kevin spent his time drinking, tossing the empty cans on the ground, and cooking the fish he had caught earlier that day.

It was about midnight when Kevin decided to go to bed; as he got settled in his camper, he thought he could hear rustling leaves as if someone or something was moving near his camp. Too tired to check it out, he shrugged it off and slept.

The following day, as he emerged from his camper, Kevin found strange markings on the side of the trailer written in what he could only guess was blood and what looked like the prints of bare human feet around the camp. After half an hour of cleaning the camper, Kevin sat by the fire pit and started drinking.

After polishing off a six-pack of beer, Kevin walked along a trail near the campsite. The woods were mostly quiet except for birds chirping in the trees. Kevin felt he was being watched as he walked but couldn't see anyone. After a while, he decided to head back to camp. As he turned, he saw a young woman with tanned skin, long dirty black hair, blue eyes, and animal furs for clothes. She was staring at him. Startled, Kevin broke into a run, following the trail back to his camp, matched step by step by the creepy woman in furs.

As he passed the tree line and returned to his campsite, Kevin fell to the ground, exhausted. When he looked behind him, he saw the woman chasing him calmly walk up to him, hardly seeming winded despite running after him. As she approached, she chanted something in a language Kevin didn't understand.

Kevin wanted to get up and run, but his legs wouldn't move, and he found he couldn't look away from the woman, who was now standing right over him. The stench of death hung thick from the furs she wore.

As Keven looked into her eyes, he felt a sharp pain throughout his entire body and passed out.

Weeks passed, and Kevin was never seen again. The only evidence he had been at the campsite was the camper and the beer cans he had left all over. Occasionally, visitors to those woods claim to glimpse the woman in furs, a large gray wolf with red eyes always at her side.

11

the Beast in the Darkness

It was the first day of classes at Thomas' middle school after spring break in Sonora, California. The sun was out, there was a gentle breeze outside, and Thomas was sitting at his desk eagerly awaiting the bell to signal the end of the day. After an eternity of listening to his biology teacher's lecture on microorganisms, the bell finally rang. Without hesitation, he got up, grabbed his backpack, and ran out the door. As he went through the school halls, he overheard some students talking about mysterious disappearances over spring break, only for the missing people to turn up dead a day later in the woods, looking like some animal had eaten them. Putting it out of his mind, Thomas left the school and went home.

When he arrived home, Thomas went to his room and started working on his homework so he wouldn't have to do it later. A couple of hours had passed by the time he finished his homework, and Tomas began to feel hungry, so he went to the kitchen, heated up some leftovers from last night's dinner, and returned to his room to eat and relax. As he ate, he remembered the conversation he overheard about the disappearances and the people turning up dead. Deciding to forget about it for the night, he went into the kitchen to put his plate in the dishwasher and then went to bed.

The following day after school, Thomas started thinking about the spring break deaths again. After finishing his homework, he looked up articles about them online. The articles he found said the victims looked like a large animal had been eating the bodies. From the bite marks they could see, they theorized it was some wolf-like animal, but experts denied the presence of any wolves large enough to inflict such damage in the surrounding area. After finishing the article, Thomas sat thinking for a few minutes, then decided to go to the woods that weekend after dark to check it out.

Saturday came, and as he had planned, Thomas waited for his parents to fall asleep, then sneaked out of the house and headed for the woods. Fortunately, he didn't live far so it only took him twenty minutes on his bike to get there.

After hiding his bike behind a tree, Thomas pulled a flashlight from his backpack, turned it on, and headed into the woods. After about forty-five minutes, he heard rustling and the sounds of somebody groaning in pain in the woods ahead of him. Turning off the flashlight so he would not be seen, Thomas slowly approached the sounds. When he reached the edge of a clearing, he found a person in the middle, hunched over and groaning. The moon was full that night, and there was just enough light to see that they were a young girl but still too dark to see who they were. As he watched them, they began

31

to contort, growing hair all over their body and becoming larger. Too scared to look away, he continued watching as their body began to take the form of a large wolf-like creature. Once the change had stopped, the creature stood up on its hind legs and howled. Now terrified, Thomas began to back away and accidentally stepped on a stick, snapping it under his foot. Hearing the noise, the creature spun around and looked directly at Thomas. As it did, Thomas turned and ran, trying not to look back as he ran for his life, all the while hearing the pounding steps of the beast now chasing him. Thomas was happy when he saw the edge of the woods come into view, and as he reached where he hid his bike, he noticed he could no longer hear the beast behind him; he didn't hear anything, in fact, but leaves rustling in the breeze.

When he got home, Thomas quietly entered the house, returned to his room, and went to bed.

Monday after school had ended, Thomas met up with his friend Zoe whom he had known since elementary school. On their way home, they talked and joked with each other. Just as they got to Zoe's house, she casually leaned in and whispered in his ear, "I know what you saw in the woods Saturday night" Then she smiled at Thomas, went inside her house, and closed the door behind her. Shocked, Thomas stood there momentarily, then walked back to his house.

After dinner, Thomas went to his room and sat on his bed, thinking about what Zoe had said. Was she the creature he saw in the woods that night and that had chased him? Confused and tired, he decided to forget about it and go to sleep.

The following day, Zoe wasn't at school, so after classes ended, Thomas went to her house and found her sitting on the front porch. When she noticed him, she waved and smiled at Thomas and invited him to sit with her. "Why weren't you at school today?" He asked as he sat down on the bench with Zoe. "I was just too tired today; I'm feeling better now, though," she said with a smile. After talking for a while, Thomas asked Zoe about what she said the other day when she said she knew what he saw in the woods on Saturday. Zoe laughed. "I was the beast you saw that night, oh and by the way, you were not in any danger; I was just screwing with you" Shocked by what he heard, Thomas just stared at her in silence and then said, "So you're a…you know" "a werewolf, yes, but you can't say anything to anyone, or I will kill you" the smile left her face. She now looked very serious. "but how? How could you keep that a secret for all this time?" Zoe then explained that she was born a werewolf but couldn't take a full beast form until recently because she didn't have the endurance to tolerate the change and that it does still take a lot out of her to do it. Thomas then asked how she could change when Saturday wasn't a full moon. Smiling again, Zoe explained that not all myths about werewolves were entirely true. A few hours passed, and it began to get dark, so Thomas said goodbye to Zoe and went home.

A few days later, there was a report on the morning news about another victim found eaten in the woods. Thomas didn't need to hear much to know Zoe had done it.

As Thomas was walking home after school, he saw a police officer standing outside their car, drinking a coffee. Unable to take his conscience eating at him, he went to the officer and told him everything, including the part about Zoe being a werewolf. After he had finished, the officer just looked at him for a second and said, "I don't have time for games, kid, now beat it!" unable to convince the officer of the truth, Thomas just gave up and went home.

That night, Thomas was sitting in his room playing a game on his computer when his cell phone rang. Zoe asked him to meet her out in the woods because she had something to talk about in private. Reluctantly, Thomas agreed to meet her, and as soon as his parents were asleep, he sneaked out of the house and headed for the woods.

Once he got to the place in the woods, Zoe told him to meet her; he looked around, but she was nowhere to be seen. "I know you told the police about me!" an angry voice yelled from beyond the trees. "Zoe, let me explain," Thomas said nervously. "You betrayed me," she yelled, still hiding beyond the trees. "Zoe, I—" "Enough!" Zoe screamed, cutting him off. Just then, Thomas heard her groaning in pain and the sounds of rustling in the bushes. Remembering the first time he saw her change into her beast form, he knew what would come next. He tried to run for it, but his legs wouldn't move. It was too late when he built up the courage to run. When he turned to run in the direction he had just come, Zoe, now in her beast form, leaped out of the bushes blocking the path. With no choice, Thomas turned the other way and started running for his life. As he did, he could hear Zoe bounding after him, snarling and snapping her jaws.

After a few minutes, Thomas fell to the ground, exhausted; catching his breath, he realized he didn't know where he was and just sat there listening for Zoe. He listened for a minute or two and heard nothing. Thinking he had lost her, he got up and dusted himself off. Just then, Zoe lunged at him from the bushes knocking Thomas to the ground. Now pinned to the ground by Zoe, he pleaded with her to let him live, but she just growled at him, opened her jaws, bit down on his throat, ripping it out, and proceeded to eat him.

It took three days for the search party to find Thomas' remains. After identifying him, his parents held a memorial service at the local cemetery to say goodbye and bury their son.

Made in the USA
Columbia, SC
08 June 2023

17757625R00024